KIDS' SPORT STORIES

CHEERS FOR GYMNASTICS

written by Cari Meister

illustrated by Genevieve Kote

raintree

a Capstone company — publishers for children

Raintree is an imprint of Capstone Global Library Limited, a company incorporated in England and Wales having its registered office at 264 Banbury Road, Oxford, OX2 7DY – Registered company number: 6695582

www.raintree.co.uk
myorders@raintree.co.uk

Designed by Ted Williams
Original illustrations © Capstone Global Library Limited 2020
Originated by Capstone Global Library Ltd
Printed and bound in India
982

978 1 4747 9373 5

British Library Cataloguing in Publication Data
A full catalogue record for this book is available from the British Library.

CONTENTS

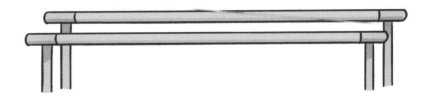

Glossary

 **floor** large, springy flat surface; during the floor event, gymnasts tumble and do flips and twists

 **high bar** tall piece of equipment that includes one horizontal bar on which gymnasts swing

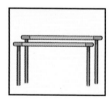 **mushroom** short, round piece of equipment used by younger gymnasts to build swinging and balancing skills

 **parallel bars** piece of equipment that has two long, wooden bars on which gymnasts swing

 **rings** piece of equipment that includes two rings hanging from a metal frame

 **vault** piece of equipment that gymnasts run towards and jump or flip over

Chapter 1

THE NEW BOY

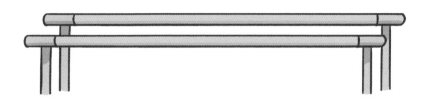

When Danny, Leo and Jordan got to gymnastics practice, their coach Charlie was already waiting for them by the door.
A small boy stood next to him.

"Boys, this is Aaron," said Coach Charlie. "He is joining our gymnastics team. He's just moved here."

Jordan and Leo smiled and said "Hi".
Danny didn't say anything. He liked
the team the way it was. He didn't want
the new boy to spoil it.

"Let's show Aaron our warm-up," said
Coach Charlie.

The boys ran in circles on the floor. They did jumping jacks and push-ups. They did forward rolls, handstands and frog jumps. Then they stretched.

Leo couldn't stretch very far, but he was getting better.

"I can almost reach my toes now!" he said.

"Look at me!" said Danny, laughing.
"I can lick my knees!"

"Danny is very bendy," Jordan said to
Aaron. "He can do the splits."

Later in the lesson, the boys saw that
Aaron could do the splits too. Danny frowned.

The boys practised on the parallel bars.

They practised swinging on the high bar.

Then they did jumps over the vault.

Danny and Aaron had the same skills. When they got to the mushroom, though, Aaron was stronger. He spun around the mushroom in a full circle! None of the boys could believe it.

"Wow, Aaron!" said Jordan. "That was amazing!"

Aaron smiled. "Thanks," he said.

Danny ran to the mushroom.

"I can do that," he said. He tried to do a circle but fell. His face went red.

Soon Coach Charlie blew his whistle. The lesson was over.

"On Wednesday, we'll get ready for the Winter Challenge," he said. "Prepare to work hard!"

Chapter 2
TIME OUT

Coach Charlie explained the Winter Challenge to the boys.

"The gymnastics competition is on Saturday," he said. "You will each compete in all six events. There will be real judges."

"Will there be ribbons?" asked Danny. "I want blue ribbons!"

"Yes," said Coach Charlie. "But remember, the competition is not just about what you can do. It's also about cheering on your teammates."

All the boys nodded, except Danny.

After warming up, the boys started on the floor. They practised the first pass. It was a handstand into a forward roll, two cartwheels and a backward roll.

"Point your toes!" Coach Charlie reminded them.

Coach Charlie showed everyone how to do the second pass. It ended with a flip.

"I can't do that flip," said Jordan.

"Me neither!" said Leo.

"I can!" shouted Danny. "Watch me!"

Danny ran out onto the floor.

"Watch out!" shouted Coach Charlie.

Danny wasn't listening – or looking. He crashed into a girl from another class.

"Danny!" Coach Charlie said. "You have to be careful in the gym. You could have really hurt someone. Time out!"

Danny sat and watched as Aaron did the second pass perfectly – even the flip. Everyone cheered, except Danny. Ten minutes later, Danny rejoined the team.

Rings were next. Danny did the routine well. He even landed with both feet together.

"Brilliant landing!" Aaron said to Danny. He put his hand up for a high five.

Danny walked past. He didn't say anything. He didn't high-five Aaron.

Jordan whispered in Danny's ear. "Why are you being so miserable?" Jordan asked. "Aaron's great."

Danny sighed. "Why does he have to be so good at everything?" he asked. "I'm supposed to be the best on this team."

"No one person makes a team, Danny," Jordan said. "Remember what Coach said. The team's strongest when we all cheer each other on. Aaron doesn't make you weaker. He makes the team stronger!"

Danny knew Jordan was right. He had to show he could be a good teammate.

Chapter 3

THE WINTER CHALLENGE

It was time for the Winter Challenge. The gym looked like the North Pole. Snowflakes hung from the ceiling. The judges were wearing reindeer antlers.

Danny went first on floor. He started well, but then he tripped and fell.

The other boys cheered him on, especially Aaron. "It's OK! Finish strong!" they shouted.

When Danny had finished, he sat down and wiped away a tear. Aaron gave him a thumbs-up. Danny gave him a small smile.

Jordan and Leo went next. Aaron went last. He did well. Danny clapped.

After floor, the boys did parallel bars, vault, high bar and rings. They had some wobbles and misses. There were a couple of bad landings. But the teammates whistled and cheered each other on.

"One more event," said Coach Charlie.

"Mushroom!"

Danny went first. He took a deep breath. He put his hands on the mushroom. *Do it, Danny!* he said to himself. *Do it for the team!* With one big movement, he swung his legs round.

Danny completed a full circle! He did it!

Coach Charlie cheered. Danny's teammates jumped and shouted. When he had finished, they ran onto the mat and put their arms around him. "That was great!" they said.

"You're the best, Danny!" Aaron shouted.

Danny shook his head. "No, our team's the best!" he said. "I'm sorry for being so mean to you before, Aaron. I wasn't a very good teammate."

"Thanks, Danny," Aaron said.

Jordan squeezed his teammates tight. "I knew you two would get on!" he said.

"Three cheers for gymnastics!" the boys shouted.

HEALTHY EATING TIPS

Everyone should eat healthily, but especially if you take part in a lot of sport. Drink a lot of water and cut down on sugar. Before your practice, try one of these good-for-you snacks:

- a hard-boiled egg
- celery and peanut butter
- a small chicken sandwich
- yoghurt and fruit

Your muscles work hard when you take part in sport. Refuel your body with a protein snack. Some good choices are:

- a smoothie
- chocolate milk
- a protein bar
- bananas with peanut butter
- cheese and crackers

REPLAY IT

Take another look at this illustration. Only Danny looks unhappy when Aaron shows how flexible he is. Jordan and Leo cheer Aaron on.

Now pretend you are Jordan. Write an email to Danny to cheer him up. Explain why having a new teammate will be good for everyone.

ABOUT THE AUTHOR

Cari Meister is the author of more than 100 books for children, including the *Fairy Hill* series (Scholastic) and the *Tiny* series (Viking). She lives with her family in the USA and enjoys yoga, horse riding, skiing and watching her boys compete in gymnastics. You can visit her online at www.carimeister.com.

ABOUT THE ILLUSTRATOR

Genevieve Kote is an illustrator whose lively work has appeared in popular magazines such as *American Girl* and *Nickelodeon*, children's books, comics and newspapers. When she's not illustrating, she enjoys baking and reading at her home in Montreal, Canada. View more of her artwork at genevievekote.com.